THE GAMEPLAN

A novel based on the major motion picture

Adapted by Beth Beechwood

Based on the Screenplay by Nichole Millard & Kathryn Price

and Story by Nichole Millard & Kathryn Price and Audrey Wells

Produced by Gordon Gray and Mark Ciardi

Directed by Andy Fickman

DISNEP PRESS

New York

Copyright © 2007 Disney Enterprises, Inc.

All rights reserved. Published by Disney Press, an imprint of Disney Book
Group. No part of this book may be reproduced or transmitted in any form
or by any means, electronic or mechanical, including photocopying,
recording, or by any information storage and retrieval system, without
written permission from the publisher. For information address
Disney Press, 114 Fifth Avenue, New York, New York 10011-5690.

Printed in the United States of America

First Edition
1 3 5 7 9 10 8 6 4 2

Library of Congress Catalog Card Number: 2007922739

ISBN-13: 978-1-4231-0830-6
ISBN-10: 1-4231-0830-2
For more Disney Press fun, visit www.disneybooks.com
Visit GamePlanMovie.com

CHAPTER

ONE

It was a beautiful Boston morning. Autumn had turned into blustery winter and snow flurries dusted the city's cobblestoned streets. Winter brought with it the promise of playoff football, and the city had high expectations for its Boston Rebels and their prized quarterback, Joe Kingman.

Deep in the heart of Beantown, Joe's apartment was a shrine to the career that had made him one of the most revered quarterbacks the city could remember. Photos of Joe from childhood all the way through his amazing career filled his trophy room. Win after win was represented. All but one was his at this point. But that one was worth all the others. In a city that measures the greatness of its sports heroes by the number of championships they win, Joe still had a big goal to meet. It was the championship trophy that drove him on the field. He had an empty case ready and waiting for the day he took that one home. And he had an empty finger waiting for a champioship ring.

It was early in the morning and Joe was still fast asleep; his bulldog, Spike, lay close by. But the early morning quiet was gone in an instant when Joe's blaring alarm clock sounded and his eyes sprung open. Right away he reached for the remote control that set the scene for the day. With one touch of a button, his bedroom curtains opened to reveal a spectacular view of the city. He touched another button and music pumped into the room.

Joe barely took a moment to yawn and stretch before heading to the kitchen for his morning shake. He blended the vegetable concoction vigorously and then chugged it in one giant gulp. Moments later, he dove into his rigorous workout routine—pull-ups, push-ups, and sit-ups, hundreds of them—grunting his one and only mantra on every exhale: "Never . . . say . . . no!"

This regimen didn't stop at home. Today was a game day, so when he arrived at Gillette Stadium— just a hop, skip, and a jump from his apartment— the sit-ups continued with music pumping through the locker room. Then, he slapped tape on his wrists, smudged black under his eyes, and slammed on his pads. He was ready for war.

And on the field, Joe was indeed a warrior. Early in the game, while running a bootleg around New York's defense, Joe evaded several tacklers, and dove headfirst into the end zone. Touchdown! The crowd erupted, just the music Joe needed for his cocky end-zone victory dance. Turning toward the cheering crowd, he led them in his familiar battle cry, *"Never say no, Joe!"*

But by the end of the fourth quarter, things weren't looking quite as promising. The scoreboard read: NEW YORK: 20, BOSTON: 14. TV commentator Marv Albert, the announcer, told viewers throughout the country that, "Boston, led by quarterback Joe Kingman, jumped out to an early lead, but it's been all New York since—scoring twenty unanswered points in the second half. Boomer, can Boston pull this out in the final minute?"

His coannouncer, the legendary retired quarterback Boomer Esiason, laid it on the line. "If they win, this will be Kingman's defining moment, Marv. If not—they'll need an Oakland loss just to squeak into the playoffs. Kingman's got to make the plays."

Down on the field, Joe took the snap and dropped into the pocket. But a huge New York linebacker made his way past Webber, one of Boston's running backs who was blocking on the play, and took Joe down—hard. A time-out was called, and Joe got right up and charged into the huddle.

Grabbing Webber's face mask, he pulled it within inches of his own.

"Webber, do you have a crush on number fifty-two?" he demanded.

"No, why?" Webber responded.

"It just seemed like you were trying to dance with him instead of block him." Joe turned to the rest of the team. "Now get on the King's back and let him carry you to the Promised Land! Sixty-two slot left—on go! Break!"

Back in position, Joe took the snap and eyed the field. Sanders, his wide receiver, was trying to break free in the end zone.

Albert gave the play-by-play. "Kingman drops back in the pocket. He rolls out to his left. He looks for Sanders. . . ." Joe saw that Sanders was open, but only for a split second and he didn't want to force the pass. So, instead of passing the ball, Joe saw daylight and took off running. He stiff-armed the free safety and spun to elude another tackler—this was his signature move, and it was a pretty one.

"The patented Kingman Swing!" Esiason shouted over the airwaves.

"Kingman, at the ten . . . the five . . ." interjected Albert, counting down in anticipation of a touchdown. But Joe was tackled right at the goal line. The game was over. Boston had lost.

After the game, in the tunnel of the stadium, Joe found himself fielding questions from reporters. "That was a great drive you put together at the end of the game. But what happened on the last play?" asked one, a reporter for a cable sports show.

"I did my job, but no one was open," Joe answered. "The only chance we had was for me to take off running. If I'd gotten another block there, I would've scored."

Later that night, in the cable show's studio, another announcer, Sean Salisbury, was commenting on Joe's earlier statement—and attitude. "Bold words from the Boston quarterback, Joe Kingman, in defeat. But thanks to Oakland's loss, Boston has earned the last spot in the playoffs.

We're here with Boston's head coach, Mark Maddox. Coach, what does your team need to work on to make a run at the championship?"

"There's a reason why everyone on the championship team gets a ring. To be successful, we need to play as a team. If not, I won't be seeing any of you till next season," replied Coach Maddox, a serious look on his face.

Meanwhile, at Joe's apartment, a New Year's Eve blowout was going on, drowning out the sports show and Coach Maddox's opinions. Stella Peck, Joe's agent, was on her cell phone.

"It's Stella Peck for Samuel Blake. Junior. Tell him I'm not holding. Sam! You can save the Happy New Year, because I won't be happy until all of Middle America is guzzling soda out of thirty-two-ounce cups with Joe's face on them. Right now, Joe loves you guys, he's all about Fanny's Burgers. But future championship MVPs are fickle, baby—you can't expect the hottest guy at the party to dance with the ugly girl forever. I didn't mean it like that. I'm losing you," she said, hanging up.

Unaware of Stella's call, Joe was walking a super-model named Tatianna to the door. "Are you sure you're feeling okay?" He reached out and put a hand on her forehead. "'Cuz only a fever could explain passing up a New Year's Eve with the King."

"I told you, they bumped up shoot—I have to catch last flight to Paris. But Tatianna will miss you."

"Well, the King doesn't want his Queen to miss him too much, so I got you a little something special." He stopped by the closet and reached his arm inside without letting her see in. He pulled out an ice blue leather Chanel bag.

"Chanel!" she exclaimed, unaware that there were dozens of identical bags in different colors inside that closet. Joe was all about party favors. Tatianna rewarded Joe's generosity with a kiss.

"It matches your sparkling eyes—I saw it in New York, and I couldn't help but think of you," Joe said, trying to sound sincere.

"I'll be thinking of you in Paris," replied Tatianna.

Joe smiled. This was exactly what he wanted to hear.

Later, all the guys were hanging around in front of the giant plasma television, intently playing a video game. On the television, an animated Joe was playing against New York.

"Think we're goin' all the way this year, King?" Cooper asked Joe.

Joe held up the hand not holding a controller and wiggled his fingers. "I didn't have my finger sized for a wedding ring!" Everyone around them cheered and hooted, while Sanders and Webber, who were standing back from the group, watched quietly.

"I don't know what he's so confident about," Sanders remarked. "We barely got into the playoffs."

"Joe says the regular season's for amateurs," Webber replied.

Back at the video game, the animated Joe had

9

thrown a touchdown, so Cooper wanted to change things up. "Come on, Joe. Let me 'be' you. You always get to be you."

Joe gave in and handed Cooper his controller. "Everyone should feel what it's like to be the King once in their lives," he said, smiling.

Joe got back to his guests then; specifically, two guests named Kathryn and Nichole. "My heart was pounding the whole game," Kathryn said sweetly. "I was so worried you'd get hurt."

"I was so scared I could barely watch," Nichole agreed.

"That's what I like about you two—you're always so concerned about . . . me," Joe said. He walked them in the direction of the same closet where he had gotten Tatianna's gift. He looked quickly at their eyes before pulling out two bags— in brown.

"Ooh! I love Chanel!" Nichole exclaimed.

"They match your sparkling eyes—I saw them in New York, and I couldn't help but think of you two."

Kathryn and Nichole exchanged looks and in unison said, "*Awwww.*"

This was too easy, Joe thought. But he cut the moment short when he noticed that Sanders was about to leave.

"Sanders! Past your bedtime?" he jabbed. Sanders's face fell. He had clearly wanted to escape Joe's teasing.

"It's New Year's Eve, Joe. I want to be with my wife and kids."

"Everybody's got their priorities," Joe replied. He grabbed Sanders's wallet and began flipping through it.

"What're you doing?"

"Confiscating your man card," he said with a laugh, holding up Sanders's wallet for all to see. "But I see that Maria already has." He turned to Cooper, Webber, and Monroe for props, and they willingly obliged. Handing Sanders his wallet back, he added, "Get a life, buddy."

"This ain't life, Joe," Sanders said before walking

out the door. Joe, however, just rolled his eyes and headed back into the party. Who was Sanders to tell him about life?

Cooper, meanwhile, turned to Webber. "Where can I get me a man card?" he asked.

In the wee hours of the morning, the last of Joe's guests were starting to leave. Most of them anyway. He had to practically shove the last three—Cooper, Webber, and Monroe—out the door. But when he was finally alone, he felt *too* alone. He almost went back out the door to retrieve the guys, but he stopped and looked at Spike.

"Spike!" The faithful bulldog ran up and wagged his tail enthusiastically. "Spike, do you know who the greatest quarterback of all time is?"

"*Ruff!*" Spike barked.

"But did you know that he is about to win the championship?" he asked next.

"*Ruff ruff!*"

"Just checking. Huddle up!" Joe got down on all

fours and pressed his forehead against Spike's. "Can you feel it?" he asked, his voice getting more energized.

"*Ruff!*"

"Can you smell it?"

"*Ruff!*"

"Do you believe it?"

"*Ruff!*"

"Z-slant Mississippi! On three! *HUT! HUT! HUT!*" He ran to the kitchen, grabbed a football-shaped dog biscuit and threw a long pass to Spike, who, like all good receivers, caught it beautifully . . . *in his mouth.* "Touchdown!" Joe yelled. He and Spike broke into a victory dance, but Joe deflated quickly. He wasn't a hero right then. He was just a guy alone with his dog on New Year's.

CHAPTER

TWO

New Year's Day was clear and cold in Boston. Inside Joe's apartment the remnants of his wild party were finally gone—no thanks to Joe. Rosa, his cleaning lady, and her three helpers had made it look like the party had never happened. They were packing up their things and getting ready to leave when Joe pulled out a wad of crisp hundred-dollar bills. He handed them to Rosa. "*Gracias*, Rosa. Enjoy your vacation."

When they were gone, Joe found himself alone again, and he was bored. He flipped the television on and then off, on and then off. Finally he decided to watch a tape of an ESPN special about his favorite subject—himself.

"Blessed with superior strength and agility, Joe Kingman could have succeeded on talent alone, but what really sets this future Hall of Famer apart is his passion for the game, and no one sums it up better than Joe himself."

Joe answered. *"Life holds many pleasures for me, but nothing beats the thrill of playing on that field every Sunday. Football is my life. . . ."* Joe, sitting on his sofa, mouthed the words along with himself. *"And beyond the field, nothing matters."*

"So why does that championship ring elude Kingman? Some say he's too selfi—"

Joe quickly fast forwarded through this part—he had no patience for criticism. "Blah, blah, blah. Come talk to me when you have your own action figure, Stuey." Spike shot Joe a look. He and Joe had a special connection. Joe could open up to Spike. "I know what you're thinking, Spike . . . my last chance, right? What kind of legacy will I have if I don't get that ring? None. Well that's not gonna happen. I'm gonna get that ring! And nothing's gonna stop me!" The phone rang, punctuating his little tirade. "Yeah?" Joe said, picking up the phone. It was the doorman, Larry, calling from the lobby.

"Excuse me, Mr. Kingman. I have a visitor here at reception who says you're expecting her. May I send her up?"

"I'm not expecting any visitors, Larry."

"A Peyton Kelly, sir."

"I don't know any Peytons," Joe insisted.

"A young lady, sir." Larry was trying to trigger some memory for Joe.

"Peyton . . . Peyton . . . Is she cute?"

"Exceedingly so, sir." On his end of the phone, Larry smiled.

"What are you waiting for?" Joe asked, his anger

vanishing. Maybe it wouldn't be such a lonely day after all.

"Right away, Mr. Kingman."

Joe shrugged and hung up. He turned to Spike. "Never say no." He headed over to the mirror to check himself out just as the doorbell rang. Opening the front door, he looked down the hall- way. It seemed empty. He started to close the door when he heard a little girl's voice.

"Hey," she said. Joe looked down—way down— in front of him. A little girl stood there holding a suitcase, a backpack, and a doll.

"Sorry kid. I don't do Girl Scout cookies. You don't get abs like these eating Peanut Butter Patties. Go ahead, punch me. Do it." The little girl obliged. Joe grinned. "Ridiculous, isn't it?" He stepped back and closed the door in her face. But the doorbell rang again. He opened the door once more and looked down at the little girl. "As adorable as you are, there's no soliciting in this building."

"What's soliciting?" she asked.

"Hey, I don't know what you're selling, but here's a hondo." Joe reached into his wallet and pulled out a one-hundred-dollar bill.

"I don't want any money. I want—"

Joe cut her off. "—an autograph. Sure." He went back inside to search for a pen, but he left the door standing open and the little girl caught a glimpse of Spike.

"You have a bulldog!" she yelped. And before Joe could stop her, she was inside his apartment.

"Careful, he's an attack dog!" But he couldn't fool her. She had already dropped to the floor and Spike was licking her all over.

"Yeah," she said to Joe. "He's gonna lick me to death."

All Joe could do was stand there and watch as Spike flipped onto his back and begged for his belly to be rubbed. "You know," he said, "little girls can't just walk into strangers' homes. There's all kinds of weirdos in this world. Didn't your mama teach you that?"

"Yeah," she said, her eyes still on the dog.

"Well? Where is she?"

"On an airplane," the girl replied.

"Then who are you here with?" he asked.

"My father," she said.

"Well, go get him, kid. He must be looking for you!" Joe was exasperated.

"He's not looking for me," she explained.

"How do you know that?"

"Because he's looking *at* me," she said. Joe froze. The little girl walked up to him then, a shy smile on her face. "Hi. We've never met before. My name is Peyton Kelly. I'm your daughter."

It was too much for Joe. Moving across the room, he sat down on one of his sofas. Peyton sat on one across from him. For a moment, neither of them said a thing. Then, Peyton spoke up. "You were married to my mom. Sarah. Sarah Kelly."

"Time-out," Joe said. "Sarah and I never had a kid." At that, Peyton pulled a piece of paper out of her bag and handed it to Joe.

"Here, she wrote you a note."

Joe read it out loud. *"Joe, I know this is a big surprise, but Peyton is your daughter and I need you to watch her for a month. It's an emergency. I'll explain everything when I get back. Sarah."* When he finished, Joe looked up at Peyton with an annoyed expression on his face. He was skeptical. But the little girl didn't notice. She was too busy exploring the apartment.

"You've sure got a lot of pictures of yourself in here," she said.

"I'm supposed to believe you're my kid based on this?" Joe asked. "Anyone could have written this."

"Oh yeah," she remembered, "I've also got this." She reached into her bag and pulled out another document. "My birth certificate." She handed it to him and pointed. "See? Your name is on it." Joe scanned the document and zeroed in on the part that concerned him. *Father's Occupation: Football Player.* Peyton grinned triumphantly as Joe fumbled for his phone and made a call.

"We've got a little situation," Joe mumbled into the phone. His voice was shaky.

A short while later, the door to Joe's apartment burst open and Stella marched into the living room to find Peyton sitting there. Both of them let out an audible gasp.

"Fix it," Joe said in a harsh whisper.

"Don't you think you should've told me about this?" Stella responded accusingly.

"I didn't know!" Joe shouted, though still trying to whisper.

"You didn't know you had an ex-wife?" Stella asked sarcastically.

"It was a long time ago. We were crazy in love, but too young . . . it lasted less than a year. And we never had a baby."

"For argument's sake—is there the teeniest, tiniest possibility that this child could be yours? Think hard."

"Look, we got separated . . . the divorce was final

. . . and she came to pick up some things. And then, we . . . we . . ." He looked over at Peyton and winced. "Is anyone else hungry?"

Stella's eyes widened. "Joe, when did this 'we . . . we . . . is anyone else hungry' happen?" she probed.

"Roughly . . . eight, maybe nine, years ago. Give or take. Plus or minus . . . carry the one . . ."

Stella looked at Peyton. "How old are you, kid?"

"Eight," Peyton replied.

"Congratulations, Joe!" Stella exclaimed.

"This isn't happening," Joe groaned.

Stella motioned to Peyton. "Come here, Muffin. Talk to Auntie Stella. This note says your mommy's coming back in a month, but see, that doesn't work for us. Joe has to win three games and the championship in the next four weeks. That means no one can bother him. So we're gonna have to reschedule this playdate."

"I have nowhere to go," Peyton said.

"Sure you do. It's called Mommy," Stella said a little harshly.

"She's on her way to Africa," Peyton explained.

"What kind of selfish, self-centered person dumps their kid just so she can go off on vacation to . . ."

"She's on a water sanitation project," Peyton began, "bringing fresh drinking water to the drought-ravaged children of the Sudan."

"If I had a dime for every time I've heard that one," Stella remarked nervously. "So, on her way to save the world, your mom suddenly just decided to leave you here?"

"I begged her," Peyton said. "I said, 'Why don't I stay with my father?' And she said, 'Well baby, he doesn't know about you yet.' And I said, 'Well, isn't it about time he did?' And she said . . ."

"I get it," Stella said. "So, who else can you stay with?"

Suddenly, Joe thought of something. "Sarah has a sister . . . Carmen!"

"Karen," Peyton replied.

23

"Yes! Karen! What about her?" Joe suggested.

Peyton hesitated and said quietly, "She's dead."

"Well, that's convenient," Stella said. Noticing Peyton's disgusted look, she added, "What? How do we get in touch with your mom?"

"Her cell won't work in Kassala," Peyton said.

"E-mail?" Stella asked.

"They don't have Internet there."

"Figures," Stella said, then asked suspiciously, "And how did you get here?"

"We flew to Boston together, then she put me in a car."

"And the car just magically dropped you off at some man's house?"

"Not some man. My father," Peyton insisted.

"So you say," Stella said.

"Want a paternity test?" Peyton asked angrily.

"That's a fantastic idea," Joe said with a lift in his voice.

Turning to Joe, Stella quickly pulled him aside for a private conversation. "Not in the middle of negotiating our Fanny's deal, it's not. Those things never stay quiet, trust me. If she does turn out to be yours, then you'll look like a guy who had a kid and ditched her, and you can kiss your megabucks good-bye."

"We don't even look alike," Joe lamented as he bent down and put his face side by side with Peyton's.

But Joe was wong. They looked *exactly* alike.

CHAPTER

THREE

Joe and Stella were in an emergency huddle. They needed to figure out their next play. As they talked in hushed tones, Peyton wandered around the apartment, Joe's eyes following nervously.

"Stella, I can't keep her here. I'm not qualified," he said anxiously.

"Don't panic. Just keep this quiet while I track down the mother and decide how to spin this," Stella offered.

"Fine. I'm going to practice. When I get back, you'll tell me what you've figured out."

"And who's gonna watch the kid now?" Stella asked.

"You," Joe said.

"I don't think so. Read my contract—Lie? Yes. Cheat? Yes. Steal? Yes. Babysit? Not included. Tomorrow I'll get you one of those . . . what do you call those servants who watch your children?" Stella asked.

"Nannies," Peyton said, frowning.

"Thank you," Stella responded.

"Mom takes me and Carmen to work sometimes," Peyton suggested.

Thinking the same thing at the same time, Joe and Stella yelled in unison, "You have a sister?!"

Peyton held up her doll in explanation. Joe and Stella traded relieved looks.

Moments later, Joe left the building for practice

. . . with Peyton in tow. He scowled at Larry on his way out. "I told you she was cute," Larry said with a chuckle. Joe shook his head as he waited for the valet to bring his car, a Mercedes SLR McLaren with a personalized license plate that read MOJOE. When he got in, he noticed Peyton hadn't budged. He hit a button and the passenger door opened.

"Let's go," he shouted to her.

"No backseat," she explained.

"So?" Joe asked. He couldn't imagine what the problem might be.

"If you get in an accident, the air bag will hurt me," she said.

"I don't have time for this!" Joe fumed. But Peyton didn't back down. Sighing, Joe hopped out of the car and yanked open the trunk. He grabbed a huge football helmet and plopped it on Peyton's very little head. "There," he said. "That helmet stood up to Ray Lewis—it can handle a measly air bag."

Peyton finally gave in and took her seat beside Joe, though the helmet wobbled on her head. Then right away she propped her feet up on the car's dashboard.

"Personal foul!" Joe yelled. "You can't put your shoes on Silver Arrow leather. Do you know how much this car costs?"

"Um, five hundred dollars?" she asked.

"Please keep your hands and feet to yourself," he said calmly. Peyton held her feet and hands up in midair in sarcastic compliance, and Joe sped out of the apartment garage—and right into traffic gridlock. He was annoyed, but Peyton took the opportunity to pull out her notebook and a pencil. Then she turned to Joe.

"I've got four weeks to make up for eight years, so let's get started," Peyton said seriously. Joe looked confused as she continued, "I'm gonna ask you some questions, and you're gonna give me some answers. For example, if you asked me what my favorite thing to do was, I'd say ballet.

So, what's your favorite thing to do?"

"Easy. Play football," Joe replied, anxiously checking the time on the dashboard clock. He honked at the traffic jam to no avail.

Peyton went along with her interview. "If you could save one thing in a fire, what would it be?"

"My *Sports Illustrated* covers . . . no, I know! My limited edition Joe Kingman sneakers!"

Peyton shook her head. "Who's your best friend?"

Joe paused to think about this for a good long time—maybe a little too long. Then he shouted, "Spike!"

Peyton let out a little giggle, then quickly turned very serious again. "What's the best thing that ever happened to you?" she asked hopefully.

This question made Joe rather uncomfortable and so he kept his eyes glued to the road rather than look Peyton in the eye. He quickly changed the subject. "Hey, I've got a question for you. Why didn't your mom bring you here herself?"

It was Peyton's turn to be evasive. She rummaged through her backpack and pulled out a package of cookies. She pulled one out and looked at Joe with a smile. "Want a cookie?"

"Don't try to change the subject," he said.

"But I made them special for you," she said.

"Fine," he took the cookie and bit into it. "Now, about your mom."

"I told you. It was last-minute. And she had a really short layover in Boston."

"I can't believe the Sarah I knew would let her daughter show up on my doorstep alone." He stopped to clear his throat. "Hold on. I get it. I know what's going on."

"You do?" Peyton asked nervously.

Joe started to massage his throat. He couldn't seem to clear it. "It's because she's gained a lot of weight, right? What's she pushin' now, a buck-eighty, a deuce?"

Peyton rolled her eyes.

Finally, they arrived at the stadium. They parked

and headed inside, where Joe ran for the field, leaving Peyton trailing behind. He looked back, annoyed. She didn't seem to understand that he was in a hurry. "Who do you think you are, *thome* roaming free safety? We're in a cover-two, little lady. *Thay cloth.*" Joe was speaking with a lisp, and Peyton could barely understand him.

"Are you okay?" she asked.

"Do I *thound* okay? What did you put in *thothe cookieth*?" It was getting worse.

"Milk, flour, eggs, cinnamon . . ." said Peyton, running down the list of ingredients.

"I'm allergic to *thinnamon*!" Joe yelled.

"I'm sorry," Peyton said sheepishly.

Joe stuck out his swollen tongue and pointed to it dramatically. "*Thorry! That'th* all you have to *thay*?! *Thorry!*"

Peyton reached to find some common ground, hoping that he would forgive her. "I'm allergic to nuts," she offered. But Joe was long gone. He had walked away from her and was pushing his way through a line of players standing on the sidelines when one of the public relations rep for the Rebels intercepted him.

"Hey, Joe! Don't forget we've got that publicity shoot today," he said. Joe grunted and continued on his way to the field. But again he was stopped. This time it was Coach Maddox.

"Joe, you're late. That's a five-hundred-dollar fine," he said.

"*Thart* a tab," Joe said smartly. He just wanted to get on the field. But there was a little voice coming from behind him that he couldn't ignore.

"Sorry. Excuse me. Sorry," Peyton said, making her way through the line of giant football players. Finally, her head peeked out at the players' hip level. She managed to squeeze the rest of the way through to find Coach Maddox looking at her quizzically. Then he looked to Joe.

"Uh, Joe . . . is *this* with you?"

"*This* is," Peyton said with an attitude.

"It'll be dealt with by tomorrow," Joe said firmly,

though his speech was still affected by his swollen tongue so it didn't come out quite as powerfully as he had hoped. Struggling to regain focus, he jogged to the huddle and called a play. "Red, thirty-*thix*! Red, thirty-*thix*!" he shouted.

The team struggled to understand what he was saying. "Huh?" Cooper asked.

"Hey Sylvester, what's wrong with you?" Webber joked.

Joe glared at all of them. He was completely frustrated. He started again, trying as hard as he could to speak clearly. "Red. *Thix-thy-thix*. Red. *Thix-thy-thix*." He broke then and ran into formation. Only, no one followed him. They were all busy staring at something else. It was Peyton. She had trailed Joe onto the field. He looked quizically at the team, not noticing Peyton.

"Uh, Joe? I think maybe you've got a rogue fan," Cooper suggested.

"I'm not a fan," Peyton objected. "I'm Joe's daughter," she said.

The whole team exchanged shocked looks while Joe traipsed over to Peyton. He picked her up like she was a football, and carried her to the sidelines.

"I didn't know Joe had a kid," Cooper said.

"Doesn't look like Joe knew either," Webber said.

"Poor thing," Sanders said sympathetically.

"Yeah. This will seriously cramp Joe's style," Webber agreed.

"I meant the little girl," Sanders said.

Over on the sidelines, Joe plopped Peyton down on the bench and gave her a stern look. "*Thay. Here*," he said.

"*Yeth, thir*," she shot back. Joe scowled at her, then went back to practice. While he ran plays, Peyton walked on the bench like it was a balance beam, eventually hopping off and making an activity out of jumping into a pile of footballs. On the field, Joe couldn't concentrate—he was too distracted by Peyton's constant movement. When they got into a huddle again, he called out, "Blue, eighty-*theven*! Hit the pine!" He was shouting in the direction of Peyton, but she had no idea what he was talking about. "*Thay* on that bench!" he clarified. "*Pleath!*" Peyton complied and sat down, but not before the team erupted with laughter at Joe's ridiculous lisp.

Practice finally ended and the public relations guy swarmed Joe, patting his face with powder and placing a Rebels hat on his head and a Rebels flag in his hand as a camera crew got ready to shoot. Joe put on his million-dollar smile. "*Bothon Rebelth!*" he shouted enthusiastically. But enthusiasm alone wasn't enough to mask the lisp. They made Joe do about a thousand takes before they finally gave up.

Back in the locker room, the guys were in their towels and Peyton sat facing the corner with an ACE bandage wrapped around her eyes like a blindfold. Joe was soaking in the bath—and his tongue had finally returned to normal size.

Cooper and Webber were talking quietly at their lockers. "Let's 'get' Joe," Cooper suggested.

"I'm sure now's not a good time," Webber said. "And you know Joe's off-limits."

"We could put ice in his bath!" Cooper said.

"He's in an ice bath," Webber pointed out.

"We'll put colder ice in it!" Cooper laughed, not exactly getting it, as usual. Webber just shook his head at his not-so-bright buddy. Sanders, meanwhile, made his way over to Joe.

"So . . . big surprise, huh?" he asked Joe.

"More like a safety blitz," Joe replied. They both looked over at Peyton, who was clutching her doll.

"You have a daughter," Sanders said, smiling. "You should be happy." Joe definitely wasn't happy. Overwhelmed was more like it. "I remember how thrilled I was when my kids were born," Sanders continued.

"Yeah," Joe said, "but you knew they were coming."

"Either way," Sanders said, "she's here."

This statement finally triggered something in Joe. This was real. He was a father and this was his little girl. He was in way over his head!

Just then, Peyton called out to the group.

"Can I take this off now?" she asked, pointing to the blindfold.

"NO!" they all shouted in unison.

Realizing the girl was probably bored, Sanders made his way over to her.

"What's your name, sweetheart?" he asked.

"Peyton," she said. When she saw the blank stares of the players, she explained she was named after Peyton Rous—a Nobel Prize winner.

"For what team?" Cooper asked. Peyton pulled her blindfold off and leveled the guy with a deep, dark stare.

"In medicine," she growled.

"He's not even a football player? That's stupid," Cooper protested.

"Stupid is a mean word," Peyton said.

"No it isn't," Cooper said.

"Yes it is," she said back, her voice rising.

"Quiet!" Joe yelled as he got out of the tub. "Both of you!" He made his way over to his locker. Meanwhile, Peyton turned around from her corner to find herself staring at the horrifying sight of a gigantic pair of underwear in a locker.

"Step away from the pants," a deep voice growled. Startled, Peyton spun around only to find the gigantic guy the underwear clearly belonged to —Monroe—standing before her. She backed away slowly.

"Awkward," she said.

"Those are his special underwear, sweetie," Sanders explained kindly. "He has to wear them every game, or he thinks we won't win."

"I still have a blanket from when I was a baby . . ." she paused, ". . . but I washed that."

"I'm not sure you should be looking at Monroe's special underwear," Sanders said, looking around nervously. "Or anything else in here, for that matter.

Right, Joe?" He was clearly hoping some parental duty in Joe would be triggered. But it was Joe. It wouldn't be that easy.

"Whatever you say, Pops," Joe said.

CHAPTER

FOUR

After returning from the grueling practice, Joe and Peyton found themselves standing in Joe's kitchen. Without Stella or the guys around acting as buffers, the awkwardness between them was suddenly palpable. "I'm hungry," Peyton said.

"Good," Joe replied, "because Tuesday nights we carbo-load. We're gonna do a twenty-twenty-sixty ration."

"Huh?" Peyton had no idea what he was talking about. "Do you have any Jell-O?"

41

"I'm not giving you twenty-eight grams of empty carbs. We don't eat simple sugars in this house," Joe said with authority.

"I'm a kid," Peyton explained. "Kids love sugar. The simpler the better."

"My dad didn't let me have sugar," Joe said.

"Is that why you never smile?" she asked sharply. Joe scowled. For someone so small, she had rather big comebacks.

About a half hour later, Joe and Peyton sat across the kitchen table from each other with a mountain of pasta between them. Spike sat at his own doggie table with his own serving of doggie carbs. After only a few bites, Peyton became so full she thought she might explode.

Joe looked at her with disappointment. "If you're gonna make the pros, you gotta get your appetite up," Joe coached.

She didn't respond. Peyton was staring at Joe's chin, which had a little sauce on it. "You have . . ."

"What?" he asked self-consciously. Peyton licked

her thumb, reached over, and rubbed the sauce off. He looked at her, and for a minute, the only sound was Spike chewing.

After they'd washed the dishes, Peyton changed into her pajamas and flopped down on the couch. Joe came over and tossed her a blanket. "I don't have a guest room because I don't like guests. You can sleep here." Peyton agreed, then turned her attention to the giant remote control on the coffee table.

"What's that?" she asked Joe.

"That," Joe said dramatically, "is a universal remote. It controls the world, and it's not for you to touch."

Peyton decided to test it out anyway. "What does this button do?" she asked, pushing one down. Before Joe could answer, the curtains closed, the lighting dimmed, and romantic music filled the room. "What's all that for?" she asked.

Joe took the remote from her and stumbled

through an answer. "It . . . uh . . . helps me relax."

"Ballet helps me relax. Maybe we could take a class together?" she suggested.

"Ballet?" Joe looked at Peyton like she was crazy. "Absolutely not. Come on, go to bed."

Peyton looked at Joe. "Aren't you gonna tell me a bedtime story?"

Bedtime stories weren't a usual part of Joe's playbook, but he gave it his best shot. "The Wolf blew down Grandma's house and ate Goldilocks. And something about porridge. The end."

Peyton wasn't satisfied with this. "I mean a real bedtime story."

Joe sat down next to her and started again. "Once upon a time . . ." he trailed off as he looked around his apartment for some inspiration, ". . . there was a quarterback. And he was a handsome and talented man who was loved by everybody." Peyton gave him a look. She knew *exactly* where this story was going. "But the quarterback had a problem—a team with a bad attitude. They were jealous of the love the world had for him. So one day, the quarterback pounded his teammates' faces until they cried like babies. Then the quarterback was very happy. The end." Clearly pleased with himself, Joe smiled at Peyton. But she just frowned at him.

"A bedtime story is supposed to make you feel peaceful. Here. I'll show you. Lay down," she directed Joe. Shrugging, he did as he was told. At this point, he was just happy to lie down. Meanwhile, Peyton checked her watch. "Once upon a time, there was a princess, and she had a lot of beautiful dresses. She had a pink dress and a red dress and a blue dress and a green dress and a purple dress and . . ." Spike was positively enraptured; Joe was not.

"Okay, I get it. There's a lot of dresses and they're all different colors. So what?"

"Each dress had a secret power," Peyton went on. "The pink dress, which had pink sparkles all over it, could make her fly. And the red dress, which had . . ."

". . . red sparkles all over it . . ." Joe sighed with annoyance.

". . . could make her invisible. And the blue dress, which had blue sparkles all over it, could make her tiny. And the green dress, which had green sparkles all over it, could make her SLEEP," she said in a loud whisper with great drama. Right on cue, Joe and Spike both let out loud snores. They were fast asleep. Peyton snapped her fingers to make sure. Nothing. Apparently, her plan had worked. She picked up her suitcase and dragged it into Joe's bedroom. Then, she opened it and dug out her very sparkly cell phone and hit a speed dial button.

On the other end of the line a woman answered anxiously. "Why didn't you answer when I called?" the woman asked frantically.

"Sorry!" Peyton said genuinely. "I forgot I had my phone turned off from the flight."

"I'm just glad you got there safely," the woman said. "How is it?"

"Great!" Peyton exclaimed. "The food's not so

hot, but . . ." she looked around Joe's bedroom, ". . . my room is HUGE."

"That's nice, but how's the ballet? Is it as good as they promised?" The woman clearly had no idea where Peyton was at that moment.

The reason? Almost everything Peyton had told Joe and Stella was a lie.

"Too soon to tell," Peyton said vaguely.

"Ugh. It's time for my flight. I'll call you as soon as I can. I miss you so much already! E-mail me lots of pictures, okay? I love you!"

"I love you, too. Bye." With that, Peyton hung up and opened her suitcase so that she could bury her phone . . . again. Plunging the phone deep into the stack of ballet leotards she had packed, she dug through some more until she found a shoe box. She patted it, reassuring herself that it was still there. Then, closing the suitcase, she climbed into Joe's giant bed. With her doll in her arms, she quickly fell asleep.

* * *

Peyton woke up early the next morning and got ready for the day. She put on her favorite pink ballet outfit and found a matching one for Spike. She decided Spike's outfit would look better if he had a manicure and pedicure to match. She pulled out her favorite pink polish and *voila*!

Then Peyton decided it was time to wake Joe. Using the universal remote, she turned on music and waited. Joe startled awake. But when he heard the notes of the classical piece, he cringed. He *hated* classical music.

Peyton didn't care. "Is there a ballet school close by?" she asked.

Before Joe could answer the question, Spike trotted out in front of him in his baby-pink tutu. "What did you do to Spike?!" asked Joe, who was shocked.

"He's learning *Swan Lake*," Peyton said, matter-of-factly. Spike, meanwhile, wagged his tail happily as Joe caught a closer look at his baby-pink nails.

"Spike, come here! Now!" Joe commanded. But

Spike was defiant. He seemed fond of his new look. He stood by Peyton.

"Can you French braid?" Peyton asked.

Joe glared at her. "Are you kidding me?" he asked, exasperated as he rose stiffly from the couch in obvious pain. He tried to do some back twists and neck cracks to loosen up. All of his knuckles popped.

"My mom says we're not supposed to pop our knuckles," said Peyton.

"Your mom didn't sleep on a hard sofa instead of her ten-thousand-dollar specially designed orthopedic bed." Joe stared at Peyton and cringed again as the classical music reached a crescendo. It was killing him. "What's with the . . . Beethoven?" he asked.

"It's Tchaikovsky," Peyton said.

"You say tomato. I say . . ." Joe joked.

"They're not even close," Peyton said seriously, not amused.

"Do you listen to this stuff every morning?"

"No. Sometimes I listen to Bach or Rachmaninoff or . . ."

"Do you have an iPod?" Joe interrupted rudely. "'Cuz if you don't, I'll get you one. Immediately. But for now . . ." He headed over to the stereo to turn it off, but he tripped over Carmen, Peyton's doll, on the way and tumbled to the floor. He groaned, but as he lay there, he spied something lying next to Carmen that caught his attention. "What's this?"

"My Bedazzler!" Peyton shouted excitedly. "Doesn't Carmen look pretty?" She pointed out Carmen's dress, which was covered in pink, sparkly rhinestones.

Joe couldn't even muster up an answer. He headed for the kitchen. "A Bedazzler?" he muttered under his breath. This was too much to handle on an empty stomach. It was time for his morning shake. Peyton watched in horror as Joe blended a disgusting mixture of food and poured it into two glasses. "Drink up," he told her. "You'll be running the forty in under 4.5 in no time."

Peyton recoiled and held her nose tight. "That smells worse than school food."

This triggered a thought in Joe. "Speaking of school, why aren't you in it?"

Peyton did a few pirouettes around the kitchen. "I'm on break," she explained.

Joe followed her with his eyes as she danced. He was skeptical. "In January? No you're not."

Peyton continued to twirl aimlessly. "Yes I am. I go to a magnet school and it goes year-round."

"Well, guess what—I'm *not* on break. I'm on the opposite of break," Joe said, checking his watch. "And I have to be at practice ten minutes ago."

Oblivious to Joe's growing irritation, Peyton kept spinning and spinning around the kitchen.

"So put some hustle in it. Let's go," he said gruffly. But Peyton was in her own little ballerina world. She just kept spinning and spinning, faster and faster, until she knocked into the blender. It crashed to the floor and shattered—but not before the remains of the shake flew through the air and splattered all over Joe's face. The crash finally stopped Peyton. This was not good.

But instead of screaming, Joe just looked at her, gritting his teeth. Still not speaking, Joe pulled out a piece of paper and some of Peyton's crayons and started drawing lots of x's and o's—it looked a lot like a game plan.

"Do you know what a playbook is?" Joe asked when he had finished.

"I'm guessing a book with plays." She was still a little shaky from her accident. But Joe kept drawing as Peyton looked on. "Oh," she said, seeming to have a revelation. "I get it—x's are kisses and o's are hugs."

"Wrong," Joe said sternly. "X's mean, stay out of this part of the house, and o's are for 'open access.'" He paused to make sure Peyton was listening. "This is your game plan," he continued. "Learn it." He finally finished drawing and handed the paper over to Peyton, who looked at it like it was written in another language.

Joe helped her figure it out. "For example, if you

want to go to the kitchen, it's a straight buttonhook.
The bathroom is a post pattern. No trick plays. No
flea-flickers."

"Got it," Peyton said, trying to mean it. "No
flea-flickers."

CHAPTER

FIVE

With a set of house rules in affect, Joe and Peyton headed to practice—together. When Peyton started to put her feet up on the dashboard again, Joe growled, and she quickly put them back down.

"Are you always this cranky in the morning?" Peyton asked as they sped toward the stadium.

"Only when I sleep on the couch and wake up to find my dog in a skirt," he retorted.

"It's a tutu," she pointed out.

"Yeah?" Joe asked. "Well, Spike doesn't wear tutus."

"He did today," Peyton said as she dug into her backpack for her notebook and pencil. "So," she said, returning to her interview questions, "what's your favorite hobby?"

"Winning," Joe said brusquely.

"That's not a hobby," Peyton said. "A hobby is something you enjoy doing in your spare time. So, what do you enjoy doing in your spare time?"

Joe thought about this for a minute. "I like winning in my spare time, too."

Peyton rolled her eyes, but moved on to her next question. "What's the best thing that's ever happened to you?" she asked again hopefully. Joe had avoided the question yesterday, but maybe today was the day.

"You know what I *don't* like doing in my spare time? Answering these questions." Apparently, Joe wouldn't answer that question today either.

When they arrived at the stadium, Joe headed

out for practice while Peyton paced the sidelines, looking bored. After the final whistle blew, ending practice, Stella appeared in heels with a string of young women following her out onto the field. They stood in a line as Joe jogged toward them.

Stella looked at Joe and presented her finds. "Now pick a nanny, Joe." He scanned the group and then turned to Stella.

"I'll take the—" but before Joe could finish, Sanders stopped him.

"Whoa, whoa, whoa," he said. "Aren't you going to ask them a few questions first?"

But Joe dismissed him. "I've got great instincts," he said. Then he turned back to Stella. "The one on the end."

Stella nodded and yelled out, "Edna!" A Mary Poppins-type-looking woman stepped out, and Joe winced. That wasn't who he meant.

"Whoa! Other end, Stella," he corrected.

"Blondie," Stella shouted. "You're up."

Delighted, the girl jumped up and down like a

cheerleader. "He picked me, he picked me, he picked me!" She giggled and clapped as Joe grinned broadly at the flattery. "We're gonna be just like sisters!" Cindy, the new nanny, said to Peyton, who gave a fake smile in return. There was no way she and Cindy would *ever* be like sisters.

"You start tomorrow," Stella announced before turning to speak to Joe privately. "The kid's story checks out. According to the Web site I found, Engineer Kelly is indeed working on a Sudanese water-sanitation project."

Joe seemed impressed. "Engineer? Huh. Wouldn't have guessed that. So, when is she coming back?"

"As soon as Bono parachutes in to relieve her," Stella said sarcastically. "The point is," she continued, "she's somewhere I'd never go and I can't reach her."

"Well, keep trying!" Joe urged. Turning, he and Peyton headed for the car, followed by Cooper, Webber, and Monroe.

"Hey, Joe," Peyton said. "What's a 'stat-obsessed glory hound'?"

Joe looked at the guys suspiciously. Where had she gotten this from?

"That's just trash talk," Joe said with a note of insecurity in his voice. Peyton still looked confused. "Guys who don't have the goods talk smack to make up for it," Joe added. He shot a look at his teammates. "But they don't say a peep when you hit your receiver on a rope from forty yards away."

"You're still going to the opening tonight, right?" Cooper asked, clearly eager to change the subject.

Joe was more than happy to discuss something else. "It *is* my restaurant," he answered.

Cooper glanced in Peyton's direction and then back at Joe. "Um, what about her?"

That was easy enough, Joe thought. He'd just bring her along. What could possibly happen?

The night almost went off without a hitch. Joe did bring Peyton with him, much to the satisfaction of the tabloid reporters covering the party. Peyton entertained herself by dressing Carmen in different outfits while Joe attended to all of his guests. But as the night went on, she couldn't stay awake, and finally she fell asleep on a pile of coats.

Joe hardly noticed. In fact, he was so on top of the world over the rave reviews his restaurant was getting from guests that he practically floated into his car at the end of the night. He drove away singing happily—until he glanced at the passenger-side dashboard and noticed a little footprint on it. "Peyton!" he yelled. He had completely forgotten about her. Making a U-turn, he raced back toward the restaurant.

Peyton, meanwhile, had awakened and had started looking anxiously around for Joe. She grabbed Carmen and headed toward a man who looked like Joe from behind. "Hey Joe—I thought you forgot—" Only, when she tugged on his coat and the man turned around, she realized it was not Joe at all. It was just a big guy with a camera. Right away *he* recognized Peyton as the little girl who had come in with Joe and went for his camera. At the same time, Joe raced in.

"Peyton!" he yelled with relief.

"Forget something?" the tabloid guy said with sarcastic glee as he shot picture after picture of Joe and Peyton. The man was giddy with the scoop he had just gotten.

Ignoring the reporter, Joe headed out of the restaurant—this time holding Peyton's hand.

But the next morning there was a flurry of activity. Stella arrived bright and early, newspaper in hand. The headline read, *BAD DAD!* and there was a picture of Joe returning for Peyton with a time stamp of "3:00 a.m." on it. This was not good at all.

"Yesterday Fanny's agreed to hand out your action figure with every order of fries. But do you think they're gonna want a spokesperson who forgot his child at a bar?"

Stella was fuming. Joe dropped his chin to his

chest. "Keep your eyes on the prize, kid—you can't play football forever," she noted before continuing her tirade. "Fanny's is more than just burgers and chicken fingers; it's your last ticket into the multibillion-dollar Blake empire. If you do right by them, they'll use your mug to sell everything from high-priced sneakers to high-speed Internet."

"You're gonna do commercials for Fanny's Burgers?" Peyton piped up.

"Yeah," Joe said.

"But my mom says Fanny's makes kids fat and gives them gas," she said.

"Well, your daddy's agent says Fanny's makes him fat—with cash—and she gets ten percent," Stella replied coldly. "Now, I've put together a press conference so we can do some cleanup. I'm the janitor, Joe's the mop, and Peyton's the mess."

Joe and Peyton both shot her a look at the same time. "What?" Stella asked, shrugging.

The three of them headed downstairs to find a Mercedes station wagon waiting for them outside of Joe's building. "Did you get a station wagon?" he asked Stella incredulously.

"No. You did. Say bye-bye to being the Bad Dad of Boston," Stella said. Joe and Peyton took in the car in front of them. It was plastered with child-friendly stickers that read: HAVE YOU HUGGED YOUR KIDS TODAY? and KIDS ROCK! It also had a license plate that read: #1 DAD.

Joe's face fell. Finally, however, he got up the courage to get in the car and they headed to the stadium for the press conference. When they arrived, Joe stopped to schmooze with reporters and sign autographs.

Stella took this moment to turn to Peyton. "Ready to smile pretty for the cameras?" The little girl simply scowled. "Sweetie," Stella said in a fake, sugary-sweet tone, "be a good girl and cooperate with your daddy, and Auntie Stella will get you a nice new BlackBerry with Bluetooth."

Peyton deepened her scowl. "An upgrade on your next international flight? Private Pilates

**Joe "the King" Kingman is
fierce—on and off the field.**

An unexpected visitor arrives on
Joe's doorstep—his daughter, Peyton!

Peyton buckles up *and* helmets up
to drive with Joe.

**There is no doubt Peyton is Joe's daughter—
she has the same rock-hard stare.**

Between football practice and taking care of Peyton, Joe is wiped out.

To impress Peyton's dance teacher, Joe trades his football uniform for ballet shorts.

**Monique gets a beautiful bouquet
of flowers at the dance recital.**

Joe and his bulldog, Spike, have a heart-to-heart.

No one is immune to Peyton's charm—not even Spike.

When Peyton has an allergic reaction,
Joe rushes her to the hospital.

It's the day of the big championship
game, and Joe is ready to win!

Joe wins the big game and Peyton's heart.

instruction? Facial rejuvenation?" Stella offered.

"I'm eight!" Peyton exclaimed.

"Listen up, Bratty McPain-in-the-Butt," Stella said sharply. "You'll swallow your misery and pain and whatever abandonment issues you might have and do whatever it takes to help your father!" Catching the last of Stella's little speech, Joe shot her another look. "What?" she said. "I'll pay for the therapy."

"Peyton," Joe said calmly, stepping away from the reporters. "What Stella's trying to say here is, this is crunch time. So, if something's bothering you . . ."

"Let's just keep it bottled up until after the play-offs," Stella interrupted.

"Fine," Peyton said. Joe and Stella breathed an audible sigh of relief. "On one condition . . . no nanny."

"No way," Joe said firmly.

"He doesn't have time to change your diapers. We hired a nanny, she starts today, and that's non-negotiable," Stella told Peyton.

"It's just, I'm feeling a little dizzy," Peyton said dramatically. "Everything's wooooooo. . . ."

"Dizzy?" Joe asked.

"I think it might be from that funny yellow soft drink Joe gave me last night . . ." Peyton said.

"You wouldn't," Joe and Stella both said.

"Try me," Peyton answered.

Moments later, they were standing in front of all the reporters. When the chatter in the room finally died down, Joe started speaking. "As you all know by now, I recently learned I'm a father. Clearly," he said, holding up the newspaper, "I'm still getting the hang of things." The crowd let out a collective chuckle. "But you better believe Peyton's nightclub evenings are behind her. We'll both be going to bed early from now on. So Denver, if you're watching, the King's coming to get'cha on Sunday!"

Stella groaned at the reporters' collective silence. This wasn't working out quite right.

Just then, Peyton tugged on Joe's sleeve and asked, "May I say something, please?" Joe nodded hesitantly and hoped for the best. Stella looked alarmed. Peyton pulled the microphone close and said, "Hi, I'm Peyton—the one who'll be going to bed early from now on." The reporters all sighed at how charming she was. "My dad didn't have much of a heads-up on this whole father thing. And he is still getting the hang of it.

"But, it's like everything else in his life—he *never says no*. He's teaching me that you can do anything if you've got motivation and determination. And the place where that starts," she said, tapping her chest, "is here, in the heart." Joe and Stella couldn't get over this. To top it all off, Peyton leaned over and gave Joe a big hug. "You're the world's greatest dad!"

"That was good," Joe whispered to her as they hugged.

"It's gonna cost ya," she whispered back.

Later that day, Joe found himself staring at a bunch of little girls standing poised at a ballet bar.

Peyton had said it was going to cost him, and she hadn't been joking. The kid seemed to know *exactly* how to get what she wanted. As he had no choice, Joe looked around. The only thing in the room worth watching, in his opinion, was the ballet instructor. The woman had long dark hair pulled up in a ponytail and her eyes were bright and beautiful.

"Rotate with the standing leg also, not just the working leg . . . keep your hips square!" she instructed sternly.

"Come on," Joe hissed to Peyton. "This isn't a real sport."

Just then, the instructor approached them. "May I help you?" she asked.

Joe gave Peyton a push toward her. "This is Peyton. She's here for . . . whatever this is. So . . . I guess I'll just come back in a few hours," he said.

The woman, who introduced herself as Monique, smiled at Peyton and then turned to Joe. "Class started fifteen minutes ago. And we don't accept students without an audition, which we held last month," she said.

Joe knew how to handle this. He flashed his million-dollar smile. "I'm sure we can work some-thing out. Money's not an object."

"I'm sorry, but this is a professional school, and . . ." Monique trailed off as she noticed that Peyton had made her way onto the dance floor and was mirroring the other dancers. Struck by Peyton's fire, Monique seemed to reconsider what she had been saying. "We can see how Peyton does today." She looked at Joe seriously and pointed toward a bench filled with women. "The moms sit over there," she directed.

The class continued until Monique called for a water break. "Peyton?" she called as the girls headed over to the water fountains. With Peyton in tow, she walked over to Joe. "Your technique needs some work, but you have drive, which is a very important trait for a dancer," she told Peyton.

"I'll work extrahard," Peyton said eagerly. "I really want to join your class."

"I'll tell you what. Our next performance is in three weeks. Rehearsals have already started, but if you're willing to work hard, extrahard, we'd love to have you."

Peyton lit up. "I can come every day!" she beamed.

"All day, every day," Joe agreed.

"This is a ballet school, not a child-care facility. And when we make a commitment to a student, we ask that the parents make a commitment to the school," Monique said to Joe.

"Well," Joe said, pretending to be modest, "I think you can make an exception in my case."

"Why is that?" Monique asked, not getting it.

"Don't you know who I am?" Joe asked. Was this even possible? he thought.

"No," she said.

"I'm Joe Kingman, quarterback for the Boston Rebels, number one on the field, number one in your heart? King of the Gridiron? Never Say No

Joe?" Monique's expression was still blank. None of this meant anything to her. "Never mind," Joe said.

"Don't you know who I am?" Monique asked in the same tone of voice Joe had used. "I'm the lady with the ballet school. And I don't take students full time unless I'm confident their parents will help out."

Peyton, meanwhile, had stepped away in order to snap a quick photo of herself in the ballet class.

"All right," Joe conceded. "I'll help. I promise."

CHAPTER

SIX

Between football and ballet, both Joe and Peyton had a lot of practicing to do over the next couple of days. But mostly what they ended up practicing was getting on each other's nerves. Sunday was a game day, however. Joe had no choice but to focus despite the distraction. Sooner than he would have liked, the day arrived.

"Hello everybody," said the TV broadcaster. "I'm Marv Albert, along with Boomer Esiason. We're here in the Mile High City, where Denver hosts Boston in the first round of the playoffs."

"In what should be a great showdown, we have a rematch of last year's conference final, in which Denver narrowly escaped with a 34-30 victory over Boston," Esiason said.

Up in a skybox, Peyton sat with Stella and Samuel Blake, Jr., the owner of Fanny's Burgers. The Fanny's Burgers hippo mascot was there, too, trying to force its greasy burgers and fries on Peyton, but she stopped him cold with one of Joe's signature glares.

The game, meanwhile, had grown close. Now with only thirty-four seconds left to play, Denver was winning 21-17. But the Rebels had the ball. In the huddle, Joe directed his players. "When I get in the end zone, stand back and let the King do his thing. And then you can congratulate me." Clapping hands, they dropped into formation and the game resumed. Joe stepped back to throw a pass but ignored Sanders, who was wide open, and decided to run the ball himself.

"Joe looks like he has more faith in his legs than in his receivers with the game on the line," Esiason noted as the play developed.

"Kingman's got one man to beat!" Albert said with growing excitement in his voice. "He's at the ten, the five . . . touchdown! It's all over. Boston has defeated Denver!"

"On the legs of Joe Kingman, Boston advances to next week's divisional playoffs for the second year in a row. Will this be the year the King takes them all the way?" Esiason asked.

Meanwhile, Joe danced his cocky end-zone dance, while his teammates shot him icy stares.

The next day, already back in Boston, the Rebels— along with Peyton—sat in the cafeteria of Gillette Stadium. They had music blaring and were dancing around, exchanging high fives, when Coach Maddox stormed in. He slammed his hand down on the boom box to silence it.

"You're late," he growled at them. "The meeting started ten minutes ago. Next door."

"Sorry, Coach," Cooper said quietly, "we're just celebrating our big win."

"We didn't win," the coach said. "Denver lost. What I saw out there was pure selfishness." Peyton noticed Sanders's eyes darting to Joe. "If we can't act like a team, then none of you will win anything." As the coach continued his rant, the players began to sit. Aparently the meeting was happening here and now. "The worst thing they ever did to this game was start printing players' names on the backs of their jerseys. The only name that matters is Boston. And until you figure that out, no one— and I mean no one—is getting a ring."

Scanning the room, Coach Maddox noticed that Joe wasn't taking his speech very seriously. His daughter, on the other hand, was.

"Little girl," he asked Peyton, "what happens when you don't share?"

Peyton was startled to be called on, and

answered with some hesitation. "I get a time-out," she said.

"Good answer. And you get a time-out because not sharing is . . . ?"

"Selfish?" Peyton asked.

"That's right. It seems this little girl knows a lot more about sharing than you little girls do. Come on over here," he said to Peyton. She joined him, then he picked her up and put her on the table. "Now, can you give us an example of what it means to share?"

Peyton thought for a moment. "Say you like one kind of music, let's say clas-sical, but your, uh . . . friend, likes another kind of music, let's say rock, but you only have one stereo . . ."

"But your friend bought you an iPod!" Joe interrupted defensively. Peyton and the rest of the guys stared at him. He just didn't get it.

"So you figure," Peyton went on, "maybe if I let him listen to his rock sometimes, he'll let me listen to my classical sometimes. And that way, you both get what you want. By sharing, you both win."

"Thank you," Coach Maddox said gratefully. "I couldn't have said it better myself. You must have a very smart mother." All the guys laughed at that, but none louder than Sanders. Joe, however, just rolled his eyes.

The next day, Joe was two hours late picking up Peyton from ballet. Monique decided it was time for Joe to learn a little more about his daughter's hobby, so his "punishment" was to act as an "enchanted tree" for her private rehearsal with Peyton. Joe had to spend the rest of the afternoon with a wreath of leaves on his head, "planting his roots, feeling his connection with the ground." He wasn't happy.

And things didn't get any better when he was faced with catching Monique and Peyton as they leaped high in the air numerous times during rehearsal. By the end of their practice session, Joe was actually dripping with sweat.

"Now, what were you saying about ballet not being a real sport?" Monique asked slyly. "Ballerinas can leap as high as you, but when they come down, they come down on pointe. And hold. If ballet were easy, they'd call it football."

"Yeah, right," Joe said dismissively.

"Yeah, right!" Monique said before turning her attention back to her student. "Peyton has all the makings of a professional dancer, Mr. Kingman. Talent, passion, discipline."

As Peyton continued to dance around unaware, Joe watched thoughtfully. There was some truth to what Monique had said—Peyton was an athlete. A strange feeling welled up in his chest and for a moment, he didn't know what it was. Then, it hit him. He was proud. She was an athlete, and he was proud of that.

Later that night, Peyton looked on as Joe stretched his aching muscles with his headphones on. He clearly didn't know he had company, since he was happily belting out a song at the top of his lungs. Opening his eyes, he found Peyton staring at him. He quickly took off his headphones.

Peyton had her notebook ready. "Who's your hero?"

"Coach Meyer. My high school football coach," Joe replied.

"What's your biggest fear?"

"That I never win the championship." He paused. "But I'm gonna!" he said enthusiastically. With that, he put his headphones back on and continued his stretching.

Peyton was about to pester him with some more questions when she felt something vibrate in her pocket. It was her cell phone. She nonchalantly backed into Joe's bedroom and answered the phone. "Hello?"

"Baby, how are you?" While it was good to hear a familiar voice, Peyton wasn't eager to tell more lies.

"I'm great!" Peyton exclaimed.

"I finally got to a phone. Tell me everything," she happily demanded.

"I don't know where to start," said Peyton, being evasive.

"Where are those pictures you promised? E-mail me one right now while I'm standing here. I have to see you!"

"Okay, hold on," Peyton said as she e-mailed the picture she took the other day at the Boston Ballet School. "I just sent it. So, enough about me . . . how's Africa?" She desperately wanted to change the subject. Then she heard a knock at the door and froze. She had to think fast. "You're breaking up," she whispered into the phone. "I love you!" She flipped the phone shut in a hurry, jumped on the bed, and shoved the phone under her leg just as Joe walked in.

"We need to talk," he said.

Peyton's heart began to race. Talk? Had he overheard her conversation?

"Follow me," he instructed. He led Peyton to his trophy room, which now contained a twin bed and a dresser. "I need my bed back," Joe said sitting down on the mattress. Peyton felt her heartbeat slow . . . a little. Moving across the room Peyton sat down as her father went on. "Look, P, I know I haven't been the best father . . . or dad . . . or . . ."

"You just called me P," Peyton said softly.

"So?" he asked.

"My mom calls me P."

"Uh-huh, well . . ." He wanted to change the subject. "You know the playbook I gave you?"

Peyton took the playbook out. "No more button-hooks?"

Joe shook his head and smiled. "The quarterback is supposed to know the playbook better than anyone. But you and I . . . Look, you've been playing kid your whole life. I just joined the dad team. I'm still learning the plays."

"No kidding," Peyton said lightly.

"Sometimes, the quarterback has to think on his feet—and he calls an audible." Joe grabbed some of his trophies then and used them as action figures to illustrate his point. "Like, when the linebackers are creeping up to blitz, you need to change the play in order to score. Like in life. Sometimes things come at you unexpectedly. So you gotta call an audible. You gotta figure it out as you go . . . kinda like what we're doing. Okay?"

Peyton grinned. Despite the odd speech, she understood exactly what her father was getting at. He was going to really try and be a dad—she just needed to be patient.

Still smiling, the two adjourned to the living room where they each got a side of the split-screen TV. Joe watched NASCAR highlights, while Peyton watched *The Suite Life of Zack & Cody*. After a few minutes, Peyton looked at Joe. "Joe?"

"Uh-huh?" he answered, his gaze not leaving the television.

"What's the best thing that's ever happened to you?" she asked a little shyly.

Joe turned and looked Peyton right in the eyes. He was about to answer—actually answer!—

when the phone rang. Joe ran to get it, and when he came back he told Peyton the call had been from Tatianna. She was back from Paris.

"Who's Tatianna?" Peyton asked.

"A friend," Joe replied as he rushed around. She was on her way over, and the house was filled with Peyton's things!

"A girlfriend?" Peyton asked, fuming. But Joe didn't answer. He was too busy checking himself out in the bedroom mirror. Peyton went back out to the couch and channel surfed. Only a short while later, Tatianna burst into the apartment, not even bothering to knock. Joe was still in his bedroom, so she and Peyton were alone.

"What happened to this place?" Tatianna asked, looking around at the now slightly cluttered apartment. "It's disgusting."

Peyton hated her already. "Hi. You must be Melanie. Joe's told me so much about you," Peyton said.

"I'm Tatianna. What are you?"

"Peyton. Joe's daughter."

Tatianna was horrified. "Joe's daughter? How old are you anyway? Four?"

"How old are you?" Peyton countered. "Forty?"

"I'm twenty-one!" Tatianna gasped.

"Are you Joe's long-lost daughter, too?" Peyton asked sarcastically.

Joe walked in then, oblivious to their exchange. "Tatianna, baby! Welcome back. I see you've met Peyton. I'm not sure what she's told you, but we obviously have a lot to discuss over dinner."

"Where are we eating?" Peyton asked.

"You are eating across the hall at the Jensens'," he said to Peyton. "We are eating somewhere else." He looked at Tatianna. "You'd be surprised what people will do for playoff tickets."

Joe and Tatianna dropped off Peyton at the neighbor's and were about to get into Joe's car— which Tatianna was horrified to see was a station wagon—when Mrs. Jensen came running out with Peyton close behind. "I'm sorry, Mr. Kingman, but I guess Peyton's allergic to our dog."

"You're not allergic to Spike," he said, narrowing his glare at Peyton. But Peyton just shrugged and smiled sweetly as Joe opened the back door for her. It appeared she was coming along on his date after all.

Dinner was a nightmare for everyone involved. Tatianna was mean to Peyton and overly flirtatious with Joe; Peyton retaliated by making fun of Tatianna throughout the meal. When Tatianna caught Peyton making faces at her, she leaned in close and hissed, "Listen, pippy-squeak. Let me explain something to you. You are little girl. And Tatianna is big girl. And big girls win over little girls every time. Got it?"

"Got it," Peyton answered.

Satisfied with Peyton's reply, Tatianna got up to go to the bathroom. Peyton spotted the perfect opportunity for revenge. A waiter with a full dessert cart was headed right for Tatianna.

"Oh, Tatianna!" Peyton called. She turned back to look at Peyton. "Your runway walk is fabulous!"

Tatianna puffed up at the compliment, but when she turned back around she found herself face-to-face with the dessert cart. It was too late to stop—for both. With a loud crash, the two collided, leaving Tatianna coated in frosting. She stalked back to the table and grabbed her bag.

Looking at Joe, she said, "You'll be sorry you let little brat treat Tatianna like that. Tatianna's best thing that ever happened to you, and don't you remember it!"

Joe and Peyton drove home in silence, the easy feeling from before all but gone. The moment they got inside the apartment, Joe pointed to Peyton's room and said, "Bed. Now."

"But I'm not even tired," Peyton moaned.

"I am. Go to bed," Joe said angrily.

"To think you walked out on my mama just to hang around with the sorry likes of that!" Peyton yelled as Joe started to walk away.

"What did you just say?" Joe asked, turning around.

"To think you walked . . ." Peyton started to repeat herself.

"I didn't walk out on your mom. She walked out on me!" Joe exclaimed.

"She said you were self-centered and selfish, and that everything always had to be about you. She said your head was so swollen she couldn't believe they made a helmet big enough to fit," Peyton said.

Joe was stunned. "She said that?"

"And more," Peyton said huffily.

"It's all coming back to me now," Joe said, his voice rising. "The talking, the arguing, the driving me crazy. And you know what? You're just like her."

"Oh, yeah?" Peyton said, her voice beginning to shake.

"Yeah! You think you're right about everything. Just like her!"

"What else?" Peyton dared. Now she was getting angry.

"You scrunch your nose when you're mad! Just like her!"

"Keep it comin'," Peyton said.

"You're always working on me with those big, brown eyes!" He softened his tone a little as he looked at Peyton. "Well, that's kind of cute, actually. But it's just like her!"

"More," Peyton said.

"And you get inside people's minds and mess around with them, just like her!"

"Well, at least I've got a mind, because if I didn't, I'd be just like you!" Peyton cried.

"Well, you're safe! Because as far as I can tell, you're nothing like me!"

"Good! I'm sick of it here!" Peyton shouted.

"Then go!"

"No!"

"Then what do you want from me?" Joe asked, exasperated. Peyton stormed toward her makeshift room. "Don't turn your back on me, young lady. Tell me what you want," Joe demanded.

Peyton whipped around to face her father, her eyes filled with pain. "My mom!" she said, before she slammed the door in Joe's face. Joe could hear her crying behind the door. His anger quickly faded.

"Hey," he said gently. "There's a law in Massachusetts—no crying for kids over seven. After that, they fine you—a dollar a minute. And they take the money and build prisons with it. And then they throw the blubberers in there. I'm serious. Open the door," he urged. Nothing. He got an idea. He went into his room and grabbed his guitar. He returned to Peyton's door and started singing to her.

"I don't want to see you," Peyton said from behind the door.

"Then open the door with your eyes closed," he suggested.

She did and then ran back to her bed, her eyes still closed. Joe walked into the bedroom, still singing and making up his own lyrics. When he got to the end of his song, the room fell silent. Softly, he asked Peyton to open her eyes.

For a moment, Peyton didn't move. But then, she slowly opened her eyes and looked at Joe. "There they are," he said sweetly. "Big and brown."

"Do I really have my mama's eyes?" she asked, her breath ragged from crying.

"Yep. And her crazy long eyelashes, too. Every time you bat those things there's a hurricane in Hawaii." Peyton had never heard such a great compliment. She batted her eyes at Joe for effect. "Now see? Three houses just blew away on Oahu. It's on the news." A big grin began to tug at the corners of Peyton's mouth, but then it disappeared.

"My mom said she fell in love with you because of your guitar playing. And that you sounded just like Elvis," Peyton said.

"What do you think?" Joe asked.

"I think she is tone-deaf and you sound more like a wounded moose than the King," Peyton said, finally breaking into a wide, genuine, smile. They both started laughing.

"There's the smile I was waiting for. I'd do anything to keep that beautiful smile on your face."

Peyton raised an eyebrow. "Anything?"

CHAPTER

SEVEN

To his dismay, Joe's offer to do "anything" to keep a smile on Peyton's face meant attending "Carmen Week" at FAO Schwarz. Carmen wasn't just Peyton's doll—she was every aspiring little dancer's doll. And somehow Joe had ended up chaperoning not only Peyton, but her entire dance class to the event! About five minutes after they'd arrived, Joe realized he was in way over his head and picked up his cell to call the only person he could think of in this emergency.

"Help!" he shouted into the phone as he squeezed through the tiny entrance to Carmen Land and watched the girls take off in all directions.

A short while later, Monique arrived to find Joe having tea with all the dancers and their Carmen dolls at a miniature table. When he saw Monique, a wave of relief swept over him. Within moments of her arrival, Monique had the girls completely in order, working on new hairstyles for their dolls. "Thanks for saving me," he said. "I'm out of my league here."

"Not necessarily," Monique said with a smile. "I mean, it's true that mothers are smarter and kinder and funnier and generally better at everything, but I wouldn't underestimate the power of the father."

"The 'power of the father'?" Joe asked skeptically.

"Sure. Dads are great for picking you up and dusting you off—encouraging you to do things you never thought you could. My dad took me to my first ballet class."

"Lucky for us, he did," Joe said, nodding in the direction of the girls. Joe and Monique locked eyes for a moment.

"Well, you're not that out of your league," she said lightly. "That's a pretty cute flip you've got going." She pointed to the doll Joe was holding.

"It is?" Joe said coyly. "Really? You don't think it's a little . . . frizzy?"

The next day, Joe took a lot of ribbing from the guys about his pink nail polish. He had been talked into a manicure in Carmen Land and had forgotten to take it off before practice.

Sanders came to his rescue, though. "Lay off him, guys. Not his fault. Somebody stole his man card." Joe laughed at his friend's joke. He deserved it. But it was also their last practice before their divisional playoff game against Indianapolis, and Joe had a job to do. It was time to put joking aside.

"Listen up, guys," he said. "Indianapolis claims they're going to send us on vacation. But who's about to go fishing?" he shouted.

"They are!" the team yelled.

"Who's about to go hit the links?"

"They are!"

"Who's about to win the championship!"

"They are!" Cooper called out.

The whole team shot him a look and then shouted, "We are!"

A few days later, the Rebels were on their way to Indianapolis to play the big game that would send them to the conference finals—if they won, that is.

Lucky for them, Joe's signature moves worked like magic, and they pulled off another big win. In the locker room after the game, Sanders made his way over to Joe's locker, which was open. Inside, a drawing was taped up that had lots of x's and o's and Joe, Peyton, and Spike in the center of it.

"Artwork in your locker—I'd say she's breached the final frontier," Sanders said.

"That's our game plan," Joe said.

"I especially like the x's and o's," Sanders said knowingly.

"Those . . ." Joe smiled, ". . . those are hugs and kisses." The two of them laughed. It looked like Joe was on a good streak—on and off the field.

With the Indianapolis game behind him, Joe went home and began to focus on getting himself ready for the next game . . . and on getting better at being Peyton's dad.

He and Peyton did their workouts together—with classical music pumping through the stereo. Joe had some ballet to practice, too, since he was to play the important part of enchanted tree at Peyton's recital. Between spending time together at home, at football practice, and at the ballet school, Peyton and Joe had really hit their stride. Peyton was getting close with all the guys on the team, too. They helped her learn how to catch a football and how to stand up to a defensive line. After a few days, she was strutting into practice in her own Rebels uniform, complete with black under her eyes.

The night before Peyton's recital, Joe decided to take her to the stadium for a little treat. He led Peyton and Spike onto the field as the lights popped on. "Wow," Peyton said, "it's magical."

"You're right, P," Joe said. "I kinda forgot how beautiful it is. When I was your age, I used to dream about playing football in a stadium like this. And now I do." He paused. It was as if this was the first time Joe had stopped to think about what he had accomplished and how special that was.

Peyton broke the silence. She grabbed a football and said, "I hope you brought your A game tonight! Now huddle-up!"

They played for a while and then headed home in their station wagon, complete with its new license plate, which read: PDADDY.

Before she knew it, it was the next morning. Arriving backstage at the auditorium where the recital was taking place, Peyton was both excited and nervous. Glancing around the busy room,

Peyton and Joe spotted Monique heading toward them, a leotard in hand. "Ready for your big debut?" Monique asked, handing Joe the leotard.

"Here you go, P," he said, handing it over to Peyton.

"No, Joe." Monique smiled. "That's for you."

Noticing Joe's hesitation, Peyton stepped up. "Hurry-up offense! No huddle!" she shouted.

A few minutes later, Joe and Peyton were both dressed and ready to go. Peyton took a peek out at the audience. Seeing the crowd that had gathered, her stomach flipped. She turned to Joe. "Actually," she said, "I'm not feeling that well. Maybe we should just go home." She started to take off her ballet slippers.

Joe fought the urge to head out of there with her. He wasn't exactly looking forward to wearing his tights in public. But this was his daughter's big day. They weren't going anywhere. "Did I just hear the girl who forced me to learn pirouettes give up?" he challenged Peyton.

"I didn't think there were gonna be so many people," Peyton said quietly.

"Little Miss Press Conference? Scared of a crowd?" Joe asked.

"That was fake," Peyton replied. "This is real."

"You've just got pregame jitters. All athletes get those. Even me," Joe admitted. Peyton looked at him dubiously. "Don't you think I'm scared when I look into the face of a three-hundred-pound guy who wants to kill me?" Joe asked.

"No," Peyton said.

"Of course I am," Joe said. "And it's that fear that takes my confidence and my game to another level." As Joe spoke, the fear in Peyton's eyes began to fade. "We've worked too hard to quit now," Joe concluded as he dropped his robe, revealing his costume. Peyton stifled a laugh. "I don't care how ridiculous either of us looks out there—we're going on that stage and we're dancing our *tutus* off. Because my daughter's no quitter. She never says no!"

At that, Peyton tied her ballet slippers back on. But just as the two of them huddled up to prepare to take the stage, in walked Cooper, Webber, Monroe, and Sanders. "What are you guys doing here?!" Joe asked, in shock.

"No way the team was missing this," Sanders said.

"The team?" Joe asked, as the guys headed to their seats. He peeked around the curtain to find his entire team sitting there. He panicked. "The power of the father, the power of the father, the power of the father . . ." he whispered to himself, remembering what Monique had said.

Everyone took their places onstage and the music began. Joe was awkward but enthusiastic, and Peyton danced beautifully. Even the team was impressed by the performance, since Monique had sneaked some football footwork into the routine. When the recital was over, the class received a rousing standing ovation, led by the Boston Rebels. And when Joe stood up from his bow, holding

Peyton and Monique's hands, everyone could see that he was beaming.

Joe's big moment in football came next. The day of the Miami game had arrived and Joe, exhilarated by the previous victory and everything else that was going right in his life, led the team to another victory. They were in the championship!

Afterwards, the team celebrated in the locker room. Peyton sat in her usual position, facing the corner with an ACE bandage over her eyes. In her seat, however, she danced along with the guys. Then Stella barged in with some news for Joe.

"You may be the world's greatest football player, but I am the world's greatest agent," she said to Joe.

"What's up?" Joe asked.

"All you have to do is (A) win the championship," she said, taking a long pause, "and (B) right after you win, look straight into the camera and say, 'I'm going to Fanny's Burgers.' That's it. An instant twenty-five million," she beamed.

"But Fanny's makes kids fat and gives them gas," Peyton piped up from her corner.

"Zip it before I tie another one of those things around your mouth," Stella said to Peyton sharply. Then to Joe, she said, "I'm going to Fanny's Burgers.' Twenty-five mil. Done!" Peyton stuck her tongue out at that, but Joe was thrilled anyway.

"'I'm going to Fanny's Burgers'," he said happily. "Rolls right off the tongue." Meanwhile, Peyton's cell phone started vibrating. But as she tried to grab it, it flipped right out of her hands and under one of the lockers. She'd missed the call.

CHAPTER

EIGHT

After achieving major successes on the stage and on the field, Joe decided to invite Monique to join him and Peyton for a celebratory lunch. Soon, the three of them were seated at the Barking Crab restaurant. When the main course was over, Joe and Monique sat back while Peyton began to devour a decadent dessert.

"Do you have a big game coming up?" Monique asked Joe. She really didn't know the first thing about football.

"The championship!" Peyton exclaimed.

"Pretty exciting," Monique nodded. "Not many eight-year-olds get to go to such a big event."

"Actually," Joe said a little sadly, "Peyton will be home by then. Her mom gets back from Africa in a few days."

Monique turned to Peyton. Even with a mouthful of dessert, it was clear she was sad, too. "Can't you stay until after the game?"

"No. I have to get back before she does," Peyton said without thinking.

"What did you say?" Joe had caught her mistake. "You said you have to get back before she does. Isn't your mom picking you up?"

Peyton didn't answer—she was focusing on swallowing the giant bite of dessert she had taken in order to avoid answering Joe's questions.

"Well," Peyton mumbled. Joe leaned in and stared her down.

"Peyton. Have you heard from your mom? Did her plans change?"

"Not exactly," Peyton hedged.

"Peyton," Joe demanded.

"I was planning to tell you, but you know . . . actually, it's a really funny story. You're gonna love it," Peyton said, giving an over-the-top fake laugh.

"Quit stalling," Joe said firmly.

"I'm supposed to be studying at a special ballet program this month, but instead I snuck away to come meet you." She shoved another huge bite of dessert in her mouth nervously.

"You ran away?! Is your mom even in Africa?" Joe fumed.

"About that . . . ." Peyton started to say.

"What have you done?" Joe yelled.

Everyone was looking at them by this point, while Monique tried to calm him down. "I'm sure there's a reasonable—" she said, but Joe cut her off.

"The press is gonna eat me alive!" He couldn't stop shouting. "What a stupid, stupid, stupid thing to do! Did you ever stop to think how this would impact me?" Peyton looked all red and puffy as though she were about to cry.

"Tears aren't working this time," Joe said. "You are in serious trouble."

Peyton's face got redder and redder and Monique voiced her concern. "Joe, something's wrong. Her lips are swelling. Are you allergic to something?" Monique asked Peyton.

"Nuts," Peyton managed to say.

"There were nuts in her dessert," Monique said frantically.

"Daddy?" Peyton said quietly, looking at Joe with frightened eyes. Hearing her call him Daddy for the first time, and realizing that his little girl was in serious distress, snapped Joe out of his tirade. He grabbed Peyton and tore out of the restaurant.

"The closest hospital is Ninth and Woodrow," Monique yelled after them. Joe ran faster than he ever had on any football field. Traffic came to a screeching halt as he crossed the street and headed toward the hospital, Monique following as fast as she could.

"Hold on, baby. Daddy's got you."

Peyton was gasping in his arms by the time he got to the emergency room. "Help! My daughter needs help!" he yelled at the top of his lungs. "It's an allergic reaction," he said to the doctor and nurse who ran toward them. "She can't breathe."

"Her airway's closed!" the doctor shouted to a nurse. "Ten liters nonrebreather mask. Let's get a fifty-milligram diphenhydramine IV drip. Give epinephrine 0.3 Mg SubQ. We're gonna need to intubate!" With that, they drew a curtain on Joe and he was directed to the waiting area. Monique had finally gotten there and now watched as Joe paced the room, not speaking. Just then, they heard the click of heels coming toward them. They belonged to a worried Stella.

"It was on the news," Stella said. "Do we know anything?" Joe shook his head miserably. "Okay, Stella's here. Tell me what you need."

"Her mom," Joe admitted.

Soon after, the whole team showed up with flowers, balloons, and teddy bears for Peyton. Sanders headed right for Joe and put his arm around him. "You'll get through this. Peyton's gonna be okay. And we're gonna be with you every step of the way."

Everyone was seated when the doctor appeared at last. "Peyton Kelly's father?" she asked.

"I'm Peyton's dad," Joe said, standing and then rushing toward her.

"Your daughter is responding well to treatment. We're going to keep her overnight, just to be sure. But she's going to be fine." The whole room erupted in cheers; but the doctor pulled Joe aside to say one more thing. "You need to know about your child's allergies. It's one of your responsibilities as a father."

Joe nodded.

Just then, a strong voice pierced through the air, startling Joe. "Please tell me Peyton's all right."

Joe was too upset to speak, so Monique answered for him. "The doctor says she's gonna be fine."

"You're lucky I haven't called the police," the woman shouted at Joe.

Joe finally managed to speak. "Karen?"

"I came home early and found this," she said, thrusting the BAD DAD headline at Joe. "I called Peyton a hundred times yesterday and she didn't answer, so I flew out here, got off the plane, and saw this on the news."

"Karen?" Joe said, still in disbelief. He could have sworn Peyton had told him her aunt had died. "I thought you were dead."

"I can assure you I am not dead," Karen said. "How did you find out about her?"

"I didn't," Joe said, very confused. "She found me. Wait, is Sarah still in Africa?"

Karen shook her head solemnly. "She didn't tell you, did she? Joe, Sarah died in a car accident six months ago." Joe looked like he had been punched in the stomach. Sarah was dead? Why hadn't Peyton told him? She must have been in so much pain and he hadn't been able to help.

When they were told they could go in to see Peyton, neither one of them hesitated. Peyton's face brightened the minute she saw Joe. But her smile dimmed when she saw Karen. Her aunt sat down beside Peyton and stroked her hair. "We got to Boston, and I handed you over to the car service . . . ?"

"I sort of e-mailed and changed the drop-off location. The driver took me to Joe's," Peyton admitted.

"And where does everyone at your ballet school think you are?" Karen asked.

"In Africa," Peyton said quietly, "with you."

Karen was clearly trying not to act too angry because her niece was hurting. "The important thing is you're all right. We'll discuss everything else after we get home."

Joe looked at Karen. "Home?" he asked.

"Yes. We'll fly out as soon as Peyton's strong enough."

"Hold on a sec," Joe said. "You can't just . . ."

Karen cut him off. "Why don't we discuss our travel plans later? Right now Peyton needs to get some rest."

Soon, the little girl was asleep. While Stella stayed with Peyton, Karen and Joe stepped outside to talk.

"Are you saying that you want Peyton to live here, with you?" Karen asked.

"Yes," Joe said. "That's exactly what I'm saying."

"You haven't even been in her life," Karen accused.

"That's not my fault. I didn't even know she existed. And we've come a long way in a short time," Joe said.

"You mean, since a month ago when you forgot her in a bar?" Karen asked.

"I'm not the same man I was . . ."

"An hour ago? When Peyton almost died on your

watch?" Karen asked. "This isn't about you. It's about Peyton. What's best for *her*. She needs to be in a stable home with someone she's known her whole life."

"Peyton needs her father. She needs me," Joe countered.

Back in the room, Stella was on her phone, her back to a sleeping Peyton. "Of course it will be a huge distraction," Stella whispered. "And ugly— child-custody fights always are . . . Joe will be dragged through the mud, his endorsements torpedoed, and who knows what it will do to his shot at the championship." Stella couldn't see, but Peyton had opened her eyes and heard all of this. She could also see the ongoing fight between Karen and Joe just outside her room.

"That's not your decision to make. Sarah appointed me as Peyton's guardian. She's my responsibility," Karen said.

"I already missed eight years. I'm not gonna miss any more," Joe shouted. "I will fight for this!"

"That would be a great thing to put her through,

don't you think?" Karen asked sarcastically. "Do you have any idea how to take care of a child?"

"I've been doing it for the past month," Joe replied defensively.

"And look where we're standing, Joe," Karen concluded.

Joe was speechless. He didn't know what to do next. Then they noticed that Peyton was awake and out in the hallway with them. Without a word, she turned and headed back into the room.

"P," Joe said cheerfully, following her. "You're up. How're you feeling?"

"I wanna go home," Peyton said as her eyes welled up.

"The doctor said you can come home tomorrow," Joe assured her.

"I wanna go home. Now," Peyton said through tears. She turned to Karen. "With you." She looked down then to avoid Joe's confused and sad look.

"Peyton," Joe said, "is this about what I said at the restaurant? Because . . ."

"I just want to go home with Aunt Karen. I never should have come here."

The next morning, Peyton and Karen stopped at Joe's to pack her things before heading for the airport. Peyton barely spoke a word to Joe. When they rode away in the cab, her face was expressionless.

Joe watched through the lobby window, his fists clenched. His daughter was being taken away and he wasn't quite sure what to do next.

Joe wasn't the only one upset by Peyton's sudden departure. Spike was a mess, too. When Joe got back upstairs, the dog was busy searching the apartment for Peyton. "Come on, boy," Joe said. "There's nothing under there. She's gone."

But Spike had found something—Peyton's precious box and her notebook. Grabbing it away from the dog, Joe sat down and opened the notebook. He winced at the unanswered question Peyton had asked him so many times: *What's the best thing that ever happened to you?* Then, he spotted something else. Tucked in the notebook was a half-finished letter from Sarah.

Dear Joe,
I have written this letter a thousand times, but I could never find the right words. . . . We have a daughter. Her name is Peyton. . . . She's like you in so many ways. Athletic. Headstrong . . . I'm so afraid you'll be angry with me and not want anything to do with her. . . . We had already decided to go our separate ways . . . I rationalized that I was doing the right thing in keeping her from you. You were just starting out in your career—a child would have been a distraction . . .

Joe dropped the letter on his lap and put his head in his hands. This was all too much. He picked up the phone and dialed Karen's home number. The first time her got the machine, he hung up. The next time, though, he left the only message he could manage.

"Peyton . . . uh, hi . . . I was just calling to say, uh,

113

hi . . . Spike misses you." The machine cut him off and Joe hung up. He felt a hand on his shoulder and turned to find Sanders; the wide receiver had heard about what had happened and wanted to help Joe. "Tell me what I'm supposed to do," Joe said tearfully.

"The only thing you can do—make sure she knows you love her and nothing will ever change that. When she's ready, she'll find you again."

"Thanks," Joe said.

"For what?" Sanders asked.

"For catching all my . . . everything I've thrown at you all these years," Joe replied.

Later that day, after a long practice, a reporter stopped Joe. "Hey, Joe. Joe. Word has it your daughter's not staying with you anymore. Is it easier to focus without an eight-year-old around to distract you?"

Joe stopped in his tracks. "She's not a distraction—she's my daughter! And I'd want her here with me even if it meant I could never play another football game again. There's nothing that I love more than my daughter."

Later that night, back home in Los Angeles, Karen and Peyton caught the candid interview on the news. Though Karen was visibly moved, Peyton's expression hardly changed at all.

CHAPTER

NINE

It was the day of the championship—the game that, before Peyton, had meant everything to Joe. TV's Marv Albert, seated in the press box of Arizona Stadium, summed it up in his pregame report. "Here we are for the biggest game of the year as the two biggest rivals in football square off for their chance to etch their names in history."

"The question is," Boomer Esiason chimed in, "will Joe Kingman finally get a chance to etch his name in football history, or will New York win its third title in the last four years?"

The tension in the locker room, meantime, was thick, and though Joe went through the motions of his pregame ritual, his heart wasn't really in it. This became even more obvious when the game started with an incomplete pass by Joe that was then followed by a fumble.

"Kingman is way off his game today," Albert said as the minutes ticked by. "This is not the same Boston team we've seen march through the playoffs."

"In addition to being sacked four times, Joe's been missing wide-open receivers all afternoon. He's all over the place," Esiason noted.

Stella, meanwhile, was watching the game from a skybox with Samuel Blake. A Fanny's Burgers feast was spread out in front of them. When Blake mentioned that Joe wasn't looking that good, Stella decided to distract him by shoving a burger into her mouth and raving about it. But now that she had tasted them, she realized that Peyton might have been on to something: the burgers really were . . . gross.

Just then, back on the field, Joe got crushed by a New York lineman. Monique, who was at the ballet school watching with some of the dancers, gasped. It didn't look good. Joe was still down when the teams ran off the field for halftime. As the field cleared, everyone wondered whether or not Joe could come back from a hit like that.

In the locker room, Joe was on the training table being examined when Coach Maddox came in. "How is he?"

"It doesn't look good, Coach," the team doctor said. "He's got a separated shoulder, bruised ribs, and a severe ankle sprain."

"It's Joe's call," Maddox said. "If he thinks he can handle it, then . . ."

"I can't shake off that last hit," Joe said, his face pale with pain.

"Joe, you've worked your whole career for

this game. You want it to end in here?" Maddox pushed.

"Put Danville in—that's the best thing for the team," Joe said.

When the team went back on the field for the third quarter, Joe wasn't with them, and Blake wasn't happy.

"Sam, baby, not to worry. Our Joe's not a quitter," Stella said, with beads of sweat on her brow. She wasn't feeling so well after eating so much of the greasy Fanny's Burgers food. She definitely should have listened to Peyton on this one.

Back in a darkened locker room, Joe lay on the table in physical and emotional pain. Suddenly, the lights came on. "You got money on New York or something?" It was the only voice Joe wanted to hear at that moment. It was Peyton. Despite the pain, he hopped off the table and scooped his daughter up in a giant hug.

"Daddy," Peyton struggled to say. "Can't. Breathe."

"Please tell me you're not on the lam again," Joe said, pushing back from Peyton.

"No," Karen said, standing in the doorway. "This time she brought the warden with her."

"What are you guys doing here?" Joe asked.

"I called an audible," Peyton said with a smile. After seeing Joe on the news, the two of them had decided to catch the first morning flight to Arizona so that they could be there for the championship. "See, I thought you'd be better off without me, but judging by the butt-whooping you've got out there, I guess I was wrong. I love you, Daddy. I want to come home," she said seriously.

Joe was caught off guard. He turned to Karen, who stated, "She belongs with her father. She belongs with you, Joe."

Joe was overwhelmed. "Are you serious?" They both smiled at him and Joe reached out and pulled them in tight. This was the best hug of his life— despite the pain in his ribs.

They pulled away and Peyton looked at her

father seriously. "What are you doing in here?" she asked.

"I thought the *team* would be better off without *me*," he replied.

"I didn't travel halfway across the country to see my dad sit out the big game," Peyton challenged.

Joe pointed to his ice packs in protest. "I'm pretty banged up, P."

"Did I just hear the King give up? We've worked too hard for you to throw in the towel now. My dad's not a quitter. He *never says no*," Peyton said, her voice rising. That was all the encouragement Joe needed. Throwing off his ice packs, he headed back outside.

Through the tunnel, he and Peyton emerged with much fanfare. Danville was struggling, and fans were beginning to grow restless. Joe took in the scene for a moment. Then he kissed Peyton on the forehead and said, "I have an answer to your question, P. Win or lose today, you're the best thing that ever happened to me." Peyton stepped closer and hugged him. When they broke apart, Joe put his helmet on and headed to the field with more confidence than he'd ever felt in his life.

"Joe, Joe, Joe . . ." the crowd chanted as he approached. The King was back. Peyton ran down the sidelines and all the players high-fived her. When Joe took the field, the fans raised their "Never Say No" signs. This wasn't going to be easy. The score was 7-3 with New York in the lead, and there were just sixty-three seconds left on the clock.

"With only a minute remaining, Kingman will have to put together the drive of the century. He'll have to march the Rebels ninety-three yards with no time-outs remaining," Albert announced.

Joe ran to the huddle, though in much pain, and commanded his players to ignore the clock and focus on him. He said, "We've got plenty of time. And you know why? Because the Rebels never say no. Now, let's do this!" Joe took the snap and took off running, looking positively graceful.

"Is the King doing ballet?" Esiason asked. Back at the ballet school, Monique heard this and smiled. It looked like maybe Joe had a learned a lesson . . . or two.

Meanwhile, Joe was run out of bounds at New York's thirty yard line. One last play would have to do it. Joe took the snap and this time he spotted Sanders open. Joe broke away from a tackler and fought the urge to run the ball himself. He looked at Sanders and launched a missile that was headed straight for him—in the end zone.

"Touchdown! Boston wins!" Albert cheered.

Peyton and Karen hugged ecstatically, while up in the box Stella gave Blake a kiss on the lips. "Let's go watch my MVP take your twenty-five million, shall we?"

As Joe fought through the melee to find Peyton, he was stopped by the Fanny's camera crew. "Joe, this is it," Stella coached, mouthing the words they had practiced.

"Joe Kingman," the reporter said, shoving a

microphone in his face, "what are you going to do now?"

Joe finally reached Peyton and picked her up. "I'm going . . . to take my daughter home!" Joe said.

"Joe!" Stella groaned. But even she had to admit Joe's reunion with his daughter was priceless.

"There goes your twenty-five million," Blake said to her.

Stella looked at him and said, "I'd pay *you* twenty-five million to never eat another Fanny's Burger again."

"Daddy," Peyton said, beaming, "you won the championship."

"Peyton," Joe said gratefully, "I won much more than that."

Later that night, the only victory party Joe attended was back at his own apartment, where he, Peyton, Monique, and Spike sang and danced around the house. Joe had, in fact, won it all.